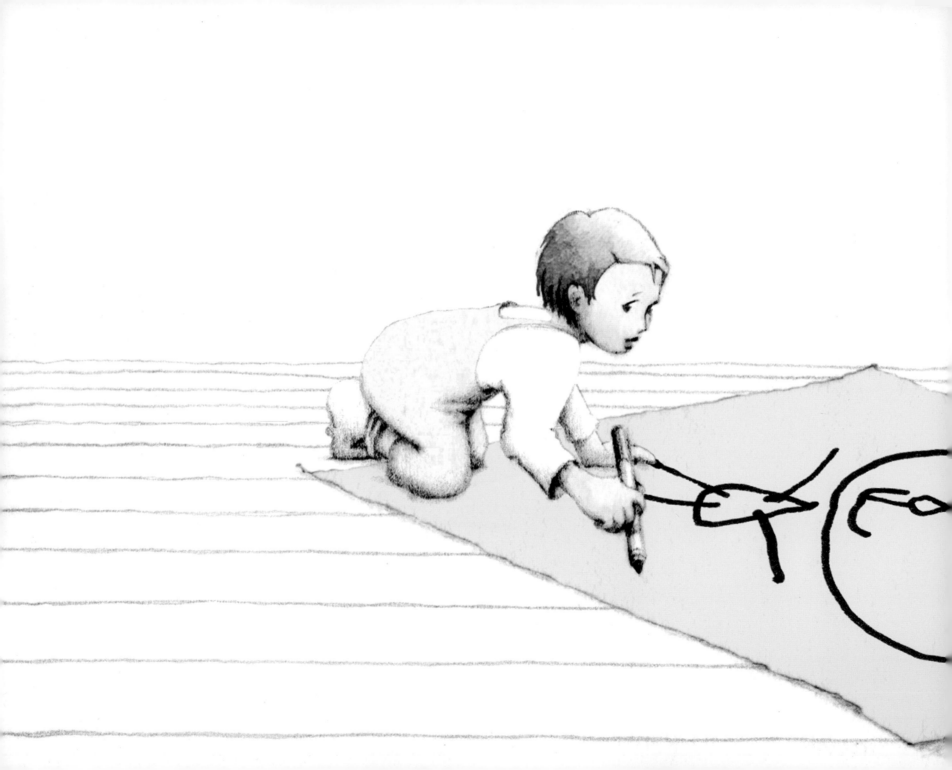

Scribble

by Deborah Freedman

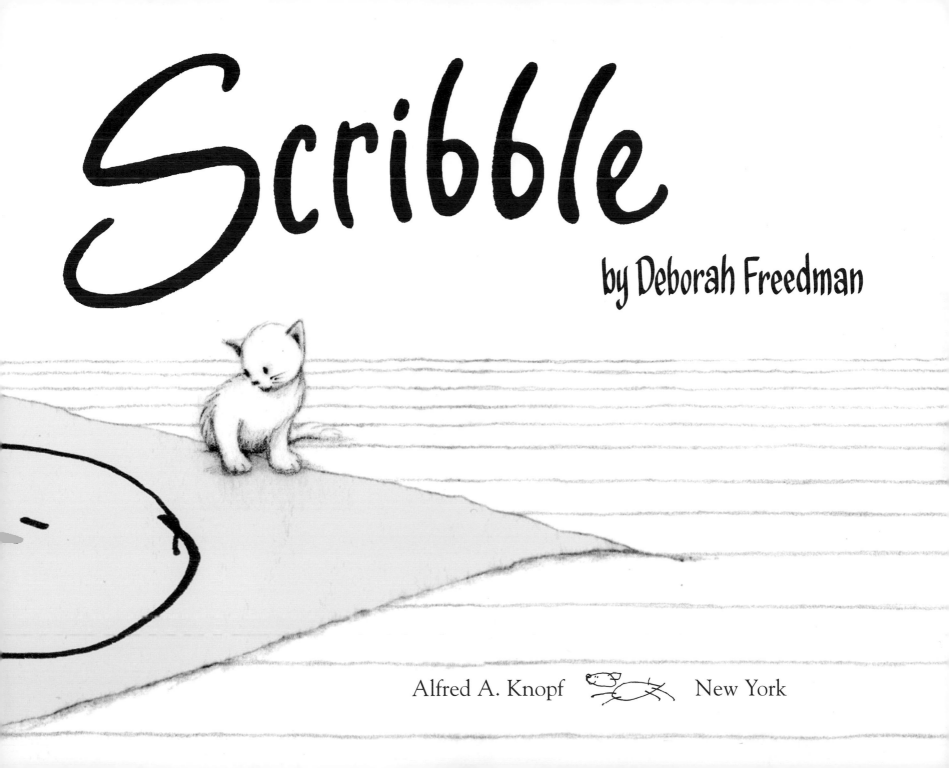

Alfred A. Knopf   New York

for Ben

THIS IS A BORZOI BOOK PUBLISHED BY ALFRED A. KNOPF

Copyright © 2007 by Deborah Freedman.

Published in the United States by Alfred A. Knopf, an imprint of Random House Children's Books,
a division of Random House, Inc., New York.

KNOPF, BORZOI BOOKS, and the colophon are registered trademarks of Random House, Inc.

www.randomhouse.com/kids

Educators and librarians, for a variety of teaching tools, visit us at www.randomhouse.com/teachers

Library of Congress Cataloging-in-Publication Data
Freedman, Deborah (Deborah Jane).
Scribble / Deborah Freedman.
p. cm.
SUMMARY: After drawing a "scribble cat" on her older sister's drawing of Princess Aurora,
young Lucie follows Scribble into the picture and tries to set things right.
ISBN 978-0-375-83966-5 (trade) — ISBN 978-0-375-93966-2 (lib. bdg.)
[1. Drawing—Fiction. 2. Imagination—Fiction. 3. Sisters—Fiction.]
I. Title.
PZ7.F87276Scr 2007
[E]—dc22
2006022733

The illustrations in this book were created using pencil with watercolors, Magic Markers, and digital coloring.

MANUFACTURED IN CHINA

May 2007

10 9 8 7 6 5 4 3 2 1

First Edition

7

And when Scribble heard that with his
new triangle ears, he grew curious.

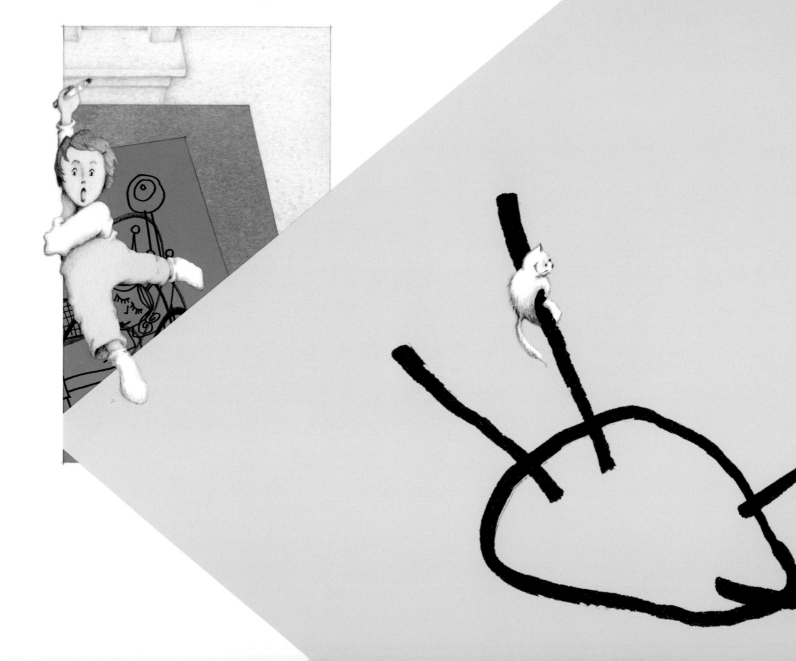

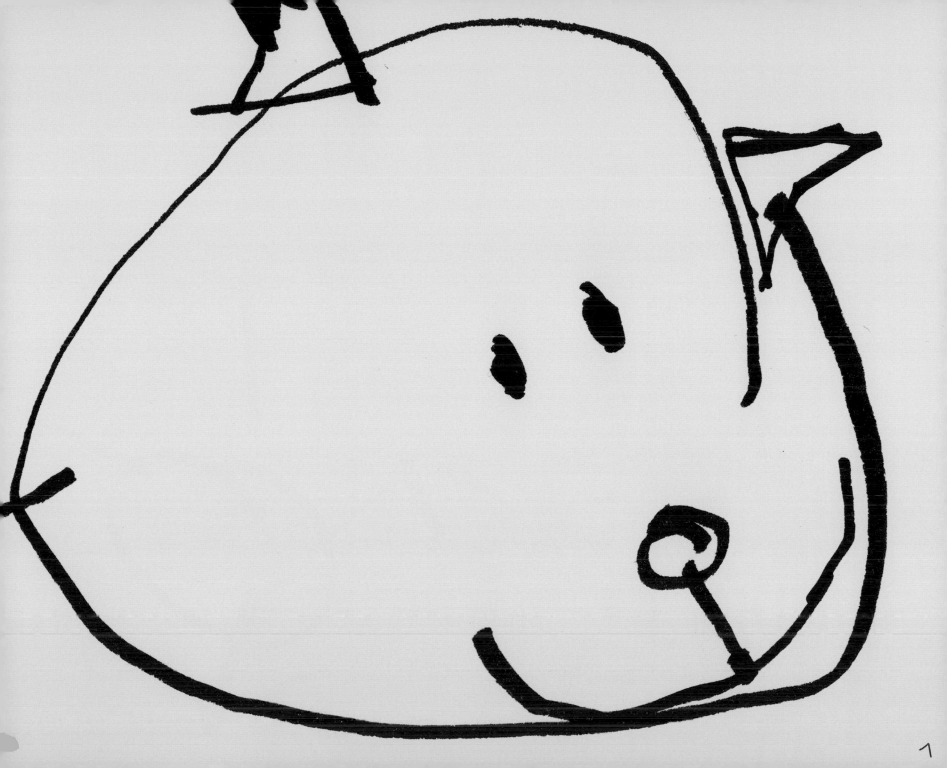

He wondered what a princess was, and he
wondered what beautiful was, and Lucie
wondered what he was wondering.

WAIT FOR ME!

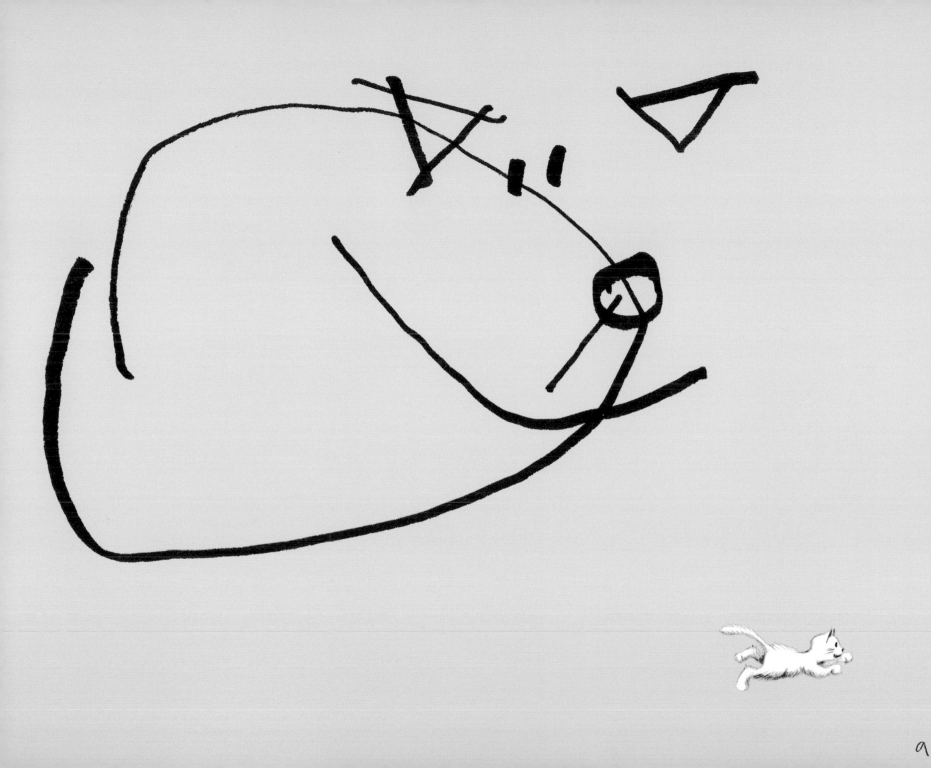

And so she followed, through
acres of one color . . .

into another, which was the color of EMMA'S PICTURE.

Then, before Lucie could stop
him, Scribble scrambled into
a Giant Thicket, where deep
within he discovered the
Princess Aurora, who had been
asleep for One Hundred Years.

13

And when Scribble saw Aurora's lovely, drowsy eyes and her rosy cheeks, he thought that she might be what beautiful was, and he longed to rescue her at once.

I'M NOT HELPING!

So Scribble began to tug.

He pulled . . .

and he struggled . . .

...SIGH...

19

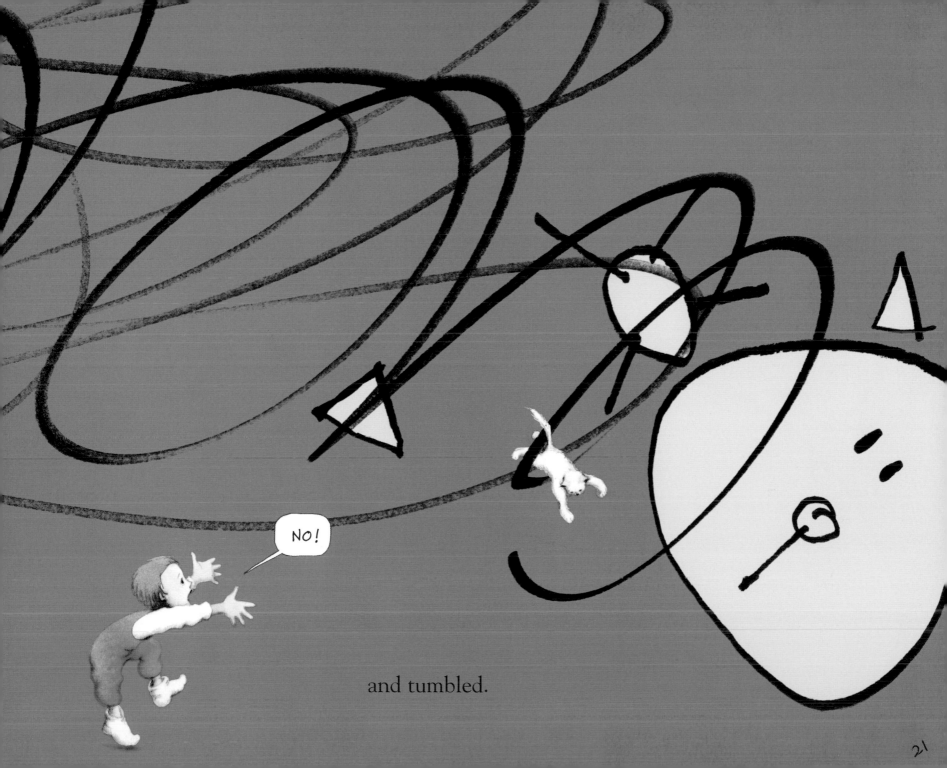

and tumbled.

And just when his heart was
nearly crushed, Scribble thought
he heard the thicket whisper . . .

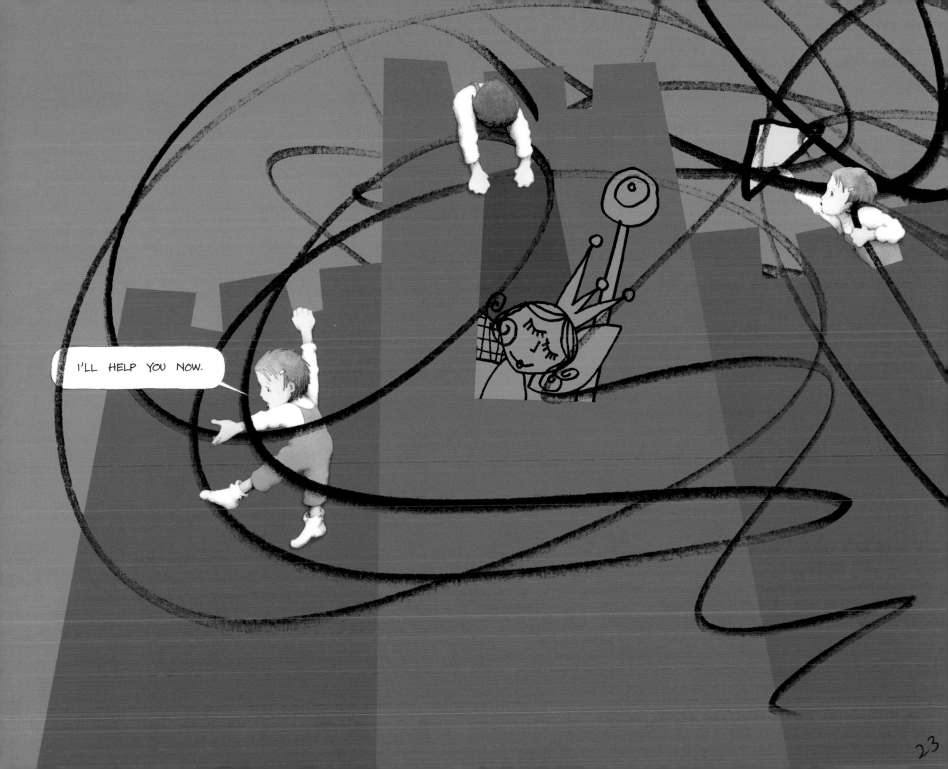

Then, at long last, Scribble
gave his princess a kiss.

And Scribble and Aurora were both so very happy they
wanted to thank Lucie and ask her to marry them . . .

. . . but before they could even turn around, Lucie was gone.

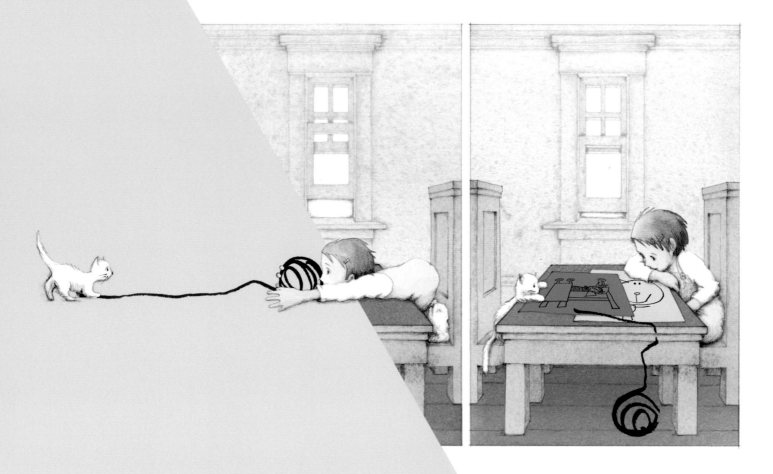

29

But they did anyway. And they all lived
Happily Ever After. As drawings sometimes do.

the end

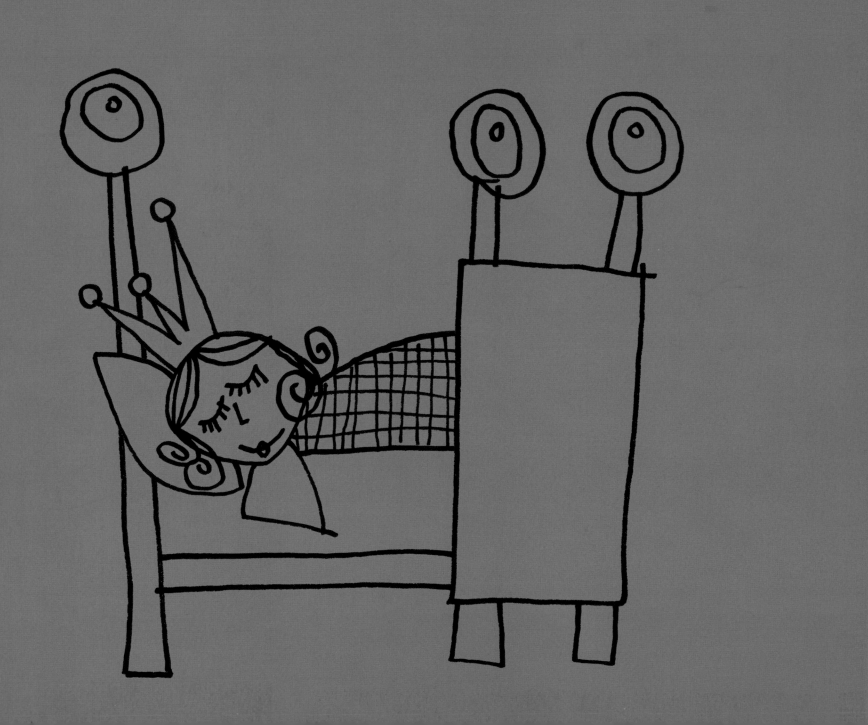